Mr. Kringle's Tales

26 Stories 'Til Christmas

Written By J. R. Cring(le)

*Except "*Bagley*" written by Justin Michael Scott (14)
Edited by Janet Scott

Table of Contents

Mr. Kringle's New Year

Having made a wrong turn on a boulevard outside Toronto and unable to get a consensus of opinion on what exit to take, a mini-van full of young door-to-door salespeople had made their way to a pristine, brick cottage in the middle of the frozen arctic tundra; having knocked numerous times, speaking to several smaller people clad in red and green velvet, aromatic of sawdust and candy.

"Excuse me, Mr. Santa. They're back again." Mandy dipped her head shyly.

"What do they want?" Santa didn't even raise an eyebrow from a well-inspected list.

"They are selling delightful weekends for two at the beautiful downtown Toronto Escaplade Hotel, complete with dinner, room, and champagne, to welcome in the New Year the right way--The Escaplade Way." Mandy closed her speech, hand raised in the air.

"Mandy, how many times have you listened to their sales pitch?"

"They seem so nice . . ."

"How many times?" Santa lifted his eyes, tweaking his mustache.

"Eleven, but actually not, because the last four I joined in because I had it memorized."

Santa stood to his feet, arching his back to release a creak, grunting. "Don't they know this is the North Pole and we're getting ready for Christmas, not New Years?"

"No," chimed Mandy. "I think they believe we are a tribe of fashion-challenged little people. They offered us a half-off special because two of us could share a shrimp cocktail."

"Shrimp cocktail?"

"I'm sure no degrading pun was intended. They're nice kids." Mandy blinked back a tear.

"I'm sure they are, but the New Year shouldn't begin after Christmas. December 1st should be the new year."

"No disrespect, Mr. Santa, but have you checked a calendar?"

"I know what the calendar says and I know what my heart says. The Christmas season is the beginning of my year. It is a time of hope and joy. It should usher in our desires for a fresh 12 months."

"So, do you want to buy a terrific package of spirits and delights from the Escaplade?"

Santa paused. "Mandy, you worry me. No. I want to start a new year, here and now. Let's start our own tradition. From this date forward, our year, here amongst the Pole People, will be December 1st--the beginning of the Christmas season."

"Wow, I think I got a chill."

"Shut the door."

"Will we need privacy?" Mandy whispered.

"No, the wind is blowing up your leotard."

Mandy shut the door, removing the chill.

Santa was stomping and hopping, ablaze with ideas. "Listen Mandy, go whip up some cinnamon-peppermint fizz punch. . ."

"You mean the zingy one?"

"That's it."

"Remember the last time we served that concoction, and two elves were AWOL for three days and Elf Randy challenged Dandy to a fight, insisting he was a wood nymph not an elf?"

Santa ignored the report. "And bake some of those cherry-holly crullers with the chocolate chip icing."

"Or as they might be called for you, STROKE-nuts," muttered Mandy.

Santa whirled around, "What did you say?"

"A stroke of genius, Mr. Santa."

"And invite those door-knockers to stay for a real New Year celebration."

The elves were gathered, and the mini-van seven stood in a circle with the Pole People as Santa lifted his cup of punch in a toast: "To Christmas, the beginning of our year. Happy Yule Year."

Everyone laughed and giggled, slurping punch and licking crullers through the night. There was glee in the North. A New Year was ushered in as Elf Randy tried to crawl into one of the logs sitting by the fire. "I and the wood are one," he slurred.

Santa's Sniffles

Let it be known: there are only two things improper, frowned upon, held in poor regard, or illegal, if you will, at the North Pole. The first is bad attitudes. An elf might be lectured and scorned if the slightest twinge of the grim were to darken the countenance. This might sound unrealistic or even harsh until you consider the nature of the business--toys, candy, confections, puppies, kittens, and colorful decorations. Anyone feeling the need to be blue in the presence of glittering red and green might deserve to be black-balled--Santa's contention. Agree or disagree, smiles and courtesy are standard fare at the toyshop.

The second dastardly, defiant peccadillo is cold germs. It was one of Santa's greatest concerns--getting a cold and being unable to deliver the toys. So anyone caught sneezing, coughing, or "talking with a noseful" was under immediate scrutiny and alienation. Because if it were confirmed an elf had the "snoots" as Santa called it, the offender would bunk with the reindeer until well. Santa was compassionate-- extra blankets, fruit, tissues, and chicken soup were provided, but quarantine amongst the beasts of the barn was the order of the day.

Well, that brings me to my story. One day Elf Dandy sneezed. The toyshop held a collective gasp. Dandy turned varying shades, all in the crimson family.

"Who sneezed?" bellowed a bass from the nearby main office.

There was a moment of silence.

"I'm waiting," continued the boomer.

"It was me," 'fessed Dandy.

"Sounds like you have a cold," said Santa, emerging from the office.

Dandy shivered and shook, quivered and quaked, and whispered, "Sawdust."

"Sawdust? You mean in your nose?' Santa queried, strolling over to Dandy's station.

All of a sudden Dandy reeled back and let off a sneeze that shook the timbers, spraying in all directions--mostly Santa's. Santa stood--surprised, drenched, aghast and agape. "I hope it was sawdust," he partially squealed, heading for his hot tea, lemon, honey, and vitamin C candy canes.

The remedies didn't work. Santa started his own sneezing and there was no sawdust in sight. He ached and creaked, dribbled and blew, coughed and chilled--the worst cold ever recorded in the history of the North Pole, maybe in all of Germdom. It went on for two weeks. Santa didn't get better. His voice was scratchy, like a runner on a sleigh racing across a tin roof. The toyshop was at a loss. All sorts of treatments were attempted. Soup, crackers, salves, ointments, vaporizers, cold compresses, hot compresses, and no compresses--nothing helped. It wasn't pretty. A runny nose on a man with a huge white beard--get the picture!

A doctor was called. Well, not exactly a doctor. He was an elf physician, accustomed to treating little workers and reindeer. After all, Santa never got sick . . . until now.

"My name is Doctor Ulandi, and you sure are a big one!" he exclaimed, placing his tiny stethoscope against Santa's huge chest.

"Vut dooz ya hearz?" Santa struggled to be coherent.

"A big boom and two little pops followed by a wheeze and a grunt."

"Izz dat goods?"

"No, you are sick, that will be twenty dollars, and please pay me before you die."

Santa gasped.

"Just kidding. I always wanted to be a comic, but didn't have the money to go to college."

Santa peered at the little medicine man.

"Got you again. Listen, you have a very bad cold and I have the cure."

"Wellz, tellz mees," insisted Santa.

"Two weeks in bed with lots of fluids," Doctor Ulandi proffered officiously.

"Id cants dooz dat. Iz hasz tooo dootz Chreesmatz."

"Then we need something drastic. I do have this old Viking cure but . . ."

"Tellz mees." Santa was desperate.

"Well, I've never used it on a blown-up person."

Santa frowned.

"I mean, I've just tried it on elves--the dosage would have to be adjusted to accommodate your . . . a . . . fullness."

Santa whimpered, "Preeez."

Ulandi agreed and began to mix the concoction. Two ground pinecones for an elf became twenty for Santa. A cup of pure peppermint elixir was a gallon for the big guy. Six earthworms, five ginger root, seven apple cores, sixteen drops of sorghum, and two cups of dried fish scales later . . .

"Now we boil it over a hot fire for three hours . . ." Ulandi stated.

After the boiling, Mrs. Claus stepped in. "This is a huge vat of mess. Is he supposed to swim in it?"

"No, drink it," deadpanned the doctor.

"Drints itz?" Santa protested through a hacking cough.

"As I said, usually I work with elves--a cup straight down and they are well." Doctor Ulandi was sympathetic but emphatic.

Santa wiggled and then he squirmed. He shuddered and then he took a deep breath, lifted the bucket to his lips and began to guzzle.

Word had spread of Santa's Elixir so all the elves scurried to view the undertaking. Gulp, gulp, trickle, trickle, slurp, slurp, groan, groan--Santa stopped once to pull a worm from his mouth-- "Dis iz gross," he whined.

"Sometimes the worms don't dissolve," Ulandi apologized.

It took a whole hour. Santa even licked the sides clean, a man determined to rid himself of the snoots.

"I think Iz feels better." He spoke much clearer.

There was a cheer, which ended abruptly. Everyone stared at the patient. Right before their eyes Santa's cheeks and nose were turning bright red.

"What's wrong?" Santa asked, staring at the astonished faces.

"It looks like you have been smeared by strawberry jam," Mrs. Claus giggled, which gave permission for all the wee folk to burst into laughter.

Santa demanded a mirror. "It looks terrible, like I kissed a can of red paint."

This caused the shop to erupt into roaring laughter.

Nobody knows what caused it--the peppermint, the ginger, the fish scales, or the less than dissolved worms. But for whatever reason, a cured Santa Claus, from that point on, had a rosy nose and bright red cheeks.

That's right. What for years has been viewed, as a trademark of the jolly old man is really just an allergic reaction to Viking Cold medicine. And now you know the whole story!

Bagley

There was once a very small boy who went to a fairly small school in an equally small town on the very big border between the United States and Canada. His name was Bagley, a most unhappy little fellow, adopted by parents who were cruel and hateful, keeping him around to do chores.

Bagley! Have you chopped that cord of wood yet?

Bagley! Run down to the creek and get water for the kettle! (Now, the creek was a good quarter-mile away, and frozen most of the year, so getting water was no small task.) He knew he was adopted because his parents reminded him—constantly." Our natural child would never look like you! Who or what could have birthed you?"

Unwanted, Bagley had no real last name, and a pretty poor first one.

Bagley's life at school was no better than at home. His clothes were tattered and his hair unkempt, but the worst thing of all--the thing he hated more than anything else in the whole world--he was scrawny and short of stature; not just a little—he was a good foot shorter than the smallest child in his school. Adding insult to injury, he had a high-pitched voice.

He was the joke of the schoolyard.

The kids made fun of everything about him, and did their best to lay all trouble at his doorstep, making the teachers suspicious of him as well.

Bagley had a secret life. Without it he would have died from simple despair—melted into a puddle like snow in the sunshine. He created a world where he escaped, deep in the woods, over the creek and across the big border (although Bagley didn't know it because there were no signs or anything). He built his own small city. Ironically, Bagley had named his creation "Canada." He wasn't sure what Canada was, or where, but the name had always represented something different to him—therefore, better.

Bagley's city was more or less a lean-to filled with all kinds of wonderful things he had carved out of the wood which he had found in the forest and discarded pieces behind the cabinet shop in the town. In the lean-to was a "store" with all kinds of candies, trinkets and goodies lying on the small counter. The treats, made of wood, couldn't be eaten, but it was fun to pretend. He even carved two people to sit at the desks in the "school"; they were his friends.

He named them Zuban and Zorna because Z was his favorite letter. He commiserated with them because they were shorter than he was. They were not dolls. Boys don't play with dolls. They were just little people who couldn't talk.

Bagley was able to escape to his little city in the woods because his keepers never questioned where he was going as long as the chores were done.

Time passed. Even his secret world paled in comparison to the dreariness of his real life, things no better. For you see, Bagley was shrinking as the other kids grew and yet another new cruelty at home—no food. There had been no meat at all the entire winter—his father staying at home in bed, coughing a great deal, and only rising, it seemed, to curse Bagley and demand more or better work.

Bagley was ready to run. He was only nine. Where would he go?

Christmas was coming--his ninth Christmas. He had never received a Christmas gift; he had heard the kids at school talking about the presents they received, but his family didn't even have a Christmas tree.

On December 24th, Bagley decided to escape to his city. It was a cold, snowy, bitter day. He brought Zuban and Zorna outside for a snowball fight. He made a pile of snowballs, and began to let fly. One went long, and hit something solid. He inched closer, trying to see what he had hit.

Suddenly arising from the mist, there was a massive sleigh harnessed to eight reindeer! Sitting in the high seat was a white-bearded, red-suited man with kind, twinkley eyes.

Kris Kringle, Santa Claus . . .at least he thought so.

Bagley had never thought much about him, but recognized him instantly. The old man smiled, and then gestured for him to come over to the sleigh. Scared, Bagley obeyed.

"Don't be frightened, fine fellow," Santa said, helping him onto the sled. Bagley was struck by how gentle he was.

"Who are you?" asked Bagley.

"Me, I think you know. But I know a great deal about you. I've investigated quite a bit in the last day or two."

"What do you know about me? Am I dreaming?"

"No, no, my friend. This is quite real. I have come to give you back your life—the one you were supposed to have."

"What do you mean?"

"I know you have not had an easy time of it, my son. But I'm going to tell you something that will make sense. Would you like to know why you are so short and why you have such a high voice?"

Bagley nodded, speechless.

Santa smiled. "You are an elf."

"A what?"

"An elf. We have been searching for you for a long time. Your parents lost you."

"Lost me? How did they lose me?"

"They were delivering presents to an orphanage one Christmas eve. They thought you were in the sleigh, but you had crawled out, and you were left there. The orphanage never realized who you were, and allowed you to be adopted. Your real parents have been searching for eight years. Well, enough of stories. Facts are, I need your help and they need you back at my headquarters."

Bagley was overjoyed. That night he and Santa traveled across the world delivering all the presents. Santa told him all about Christmas. When they arrived back at the shop in the North Pole, he saw his parents for the first time, the same size as him, if not shorter! But the clincher was when they told him his real elf name: Zandy--new name, great name--a "Z" name!

Best of all, he was part of a family!

That night, as all the elves gathered for dinner, Zandy gazed around; a room full of happy, joyful people his own size. He sniffed appreciatively. Food a-plenty—and tasty, too, judging by the smell. He glanced up and saw Santa smiling at him from the next table.

He knew then.

He was home.

❊ DECEMBER 3 ❊

Santa Does The Big Apple

Madison Avenue never quite understood Kris Kringle. He tried to explain his ideas, goals, feelings, and mission but the cash registers dinged too loudly for them to hear. Each year Mr. Kringle made a trip to New York to meet with the heads of advertising and toymaking to discuss the season's "angle" on Christmas. They registered him up at the Waldorf Astoria and he rattled around the suite ordering room service, only leaving for meetings, disguised as a janitor, departing through the freight elevator, so as not to promote a mob scene from children and the press.

This year the advertising "suits" were filled with ideas.

"Tell me, Kringle what do you think of svelte?"

"Sounds like Dutch for 'great'." Mr. Kringle attempted humor, but was stared down by a room-full of executives with expressions as wooden as their elaborate conference table.

"Svelte, Santa, svelte. A health-conscious Claus. No longer the jolly old elf. The svelte, young, athletic Norseman, trimmed beard, great hair-cut, pearly-white teeth--think Brad Pitt meets Brian Dennehy."

"Who?"

"Not who, Claus, what. What can we sell to America? Keep up. My man! Fruit snacks not candy canes. Milk and cookies are passé. Gatorade and power bars. You see, Clauser?"

"Gatorade?"

The young exec with a pin-stripe suit, close cropped slicked back hair, and tortoise-shell framed glasses, peered at the poofy, bearded, pot-bellied, long-haired, rosy-cheeked old codger wearing gray work overalls. "Santa, can I call you Santa?. . ."

"Kris or Santa, I guess . . ."

"The fire is hot, the iron is ready, the market is ripe, and the vibe is chiming, got it?"

" A . . . a chiming iron? . . ."

The young man put his arm around Kringle's shoulder. "Grandpa, it's time for you to come out of the 'Claus-et'." He turned to the room. "My God, somebody write that down!" He continued. "You're too fat! America doesn't like fat. They suck it out of their bodies. They hate blubber. Everything is FAT-FREE. Get the message? Fat is out and lean's the scene. Your day of pudgy promotion is over--kaput--athletes sell, not tubby Dutch boys. Honestly, I don't know how you got by wearing red for all those years. Black might have covered up a few rolls of the old blabbo, if you know what I mean?"

Mr. Kringle did--know what he meant, that is. So he stood sucking in his bowl full of jelly hoping for as little shakeage as possible.

"No one expects you to diet, Claus," the pinstriped critic continued. "We have contracted a four-time winner of the Mr. Universe contest--Wedge Watkins, affection-ately know to his fans as *The Walking Pec*--to do all your visuals, commercials, promo shots, you know, the 'see me' stuff."

In walked a six-foot-five-inch mountain covered in bronze human skin wearing a Speedo swim suit and. . . a . . . smile.

"How can he be Santa?" Kris objected, easing to his feet.

"We got a suit for him. Calvin Klein designed it--tight backside."

"Tight backside?" Santa collapsed in his chair.

"This is the look, Kringle. America wants beautiful not bountiful. They want hunk not chunk, buff not stuff . . ."

"I got the idea." Mr. Kringle stopped him. He heaved a sigh. "I must protest. I know Mr. Wedge is in better shape than me. I know he is a fine human specimen and probably a nice man, but . . . he's not Santa. You Madison Avenue types have all year to promote your images and beauties and muscle men. Once a year an old guy with an untrimmed beard and a fat belly needs to come along to represent the other part of the world--the average putz, if you will. I'm not pretty, God knows, I don't know what Mrs. Claus sees in me, but I am real. I am approachable. I'm not perfect; I'm Santa--all 350 pounds of me. Kids love me. You may think it's just for the toys. Maybe so, but they want their gifts delivered by an overweight toymaker with pudgy everywhere, riding in an oversized sleigh with heavy duty shock absorbers." Santa glared about the room.

Madison Avenue disagreed. There would be two Santas this year--a fat one and a flat one.

Santa went back to his suite at the Astoria, packed his bag, and prepared to leave-- back home to the North Pole where they know a Santa when they see one.

Before he left he had one more piece of business. He picked up the phone and dialed 5-3-2. "Yes, room service, I would like to order a dozen chocolate-chip cookies and a quart of milk." He hung up the phone and smiled.

The world was right again.

🎁 DECEMBER 4 🎁

The First Family

Escaping seems like such a noble adventure until the ache of retreat throbs harder, faster, heart thumping as the human soul races into the blackest night, further and further from the only light known. Then, to collapse, panting--mind whirling--perplexed, forlorn, rejected, aggravated, and weary; held closely by a lover--yet mysteriously alone.

"Where are we going?" she asked, gasping for some air.

"Away."

She waited for more, something. She needed to hear reason from his lips to comfort her unreasonable, itching frustration. "Where?" she pursued.

"Away from here." He didn't point or gesture. She knew where "here" was and why they must get away. Their hearts were dying, crushed by a cruel reality by the vicious heel of gossip grinding them to dust.

But he said no more.

Silence--like she had never heard. A sulky, forlorn, pouting childish emptiness. Why doesn't he speak? She could hear him breathe, but no words. Was he thinking? Worse--

regretting? Was he blaming her? She hated the stillness; too many story lines to fill the vacant spaces--enough to madden a saint.

"We should move," he whispered.

"Why?"

"Wolves." He stood to his feet.

"Perhaps I would welcome a wolf, a real ferocious beast to tear my flesh instead of my soul."

"People are people." He stepped away a pace, staring into the distance.

She both despised and loved his practical nature. Or was it practical? Or was it his way of stating that the gossiping neighbors were justified? She broke the solitude. "I did not lie to you."

"About what?"

"You know what! What else have we talked about for eight months? What subject has permeated every one of our meetings? It has become a life of discussion. Strategy instead of tenderness. Talk instead of kisses. Crying instead of touch. You must understand--I *did* see him."

"As did I. Still, hard to explain over wine and bread, don't you think?"

She rose, slipping, catching herself, balancing against a rock, a dull thumping throb squeezing her head. "I don't care what they think."

"Nor do I. But how can you escape what they say?"

"Is that why we're running?" All at once, there was a gurgle and leap in her womb. She released a girlish giggle.

"Is he moving again--hungry or miffed at being in the desert?"

"I think he likes it. I think he wants to play." A grunting chortle and then . . .

The silence returned. She pondered. How had she come to this--an unwed mother, claimed by a reluctant suitor, like some lame goat at an auction, pitied by the wealthy herdsman? She had a dream; that dream now stood and stared at her through the eyes of a strange man who did not totally trust her--a man she was ready to give the secret treasures of her wholeness. "Where are we going?" Same question--greater desperation.

"I had to go. I had to put us both away for a private time. Our ears needed the rest from the exercise of futility. I wanted to hear your voice, just your voice. I didn't want to hear . . ."

". . . or see. Which is worse--the words or the looks?"

"The pity or the disgust?"

"The disgust is worse. At least the pity doesn't rip a hole."

He winnowed a sigh. "I just don't know what we are going to do."

She wept.

"What is wrong?"

"I can't be strong for you. You have to be strong for you. I have barely enough faith to wrap my mind around this idea myself. I can't carry your load."

He paused, swallowed hard, and nodded.

"The tax is soon." She stared absent-mindedly at her tummy.

"We need some time. I need time with you."

"In the wilderness?"

He chuckled. "We will find a place."

For a long breath they stood together, staring at black expanses sprinkled with splotches of shimmering light. Fatigue swept over them, wooing them to their hands, knees, and then their backs.

They had found their place . . . for tonight.

They cuddled for warmth, the sand lay gently--its softest--and God shooed the wolves away.

They slept.

Mary dreamed of a baby, born chubby and pink, her child. Joseph dreamed of her, and her baby, not totally his son.

✠ DECEMBER 5 ✶

A Miracle for Elf Randy

The scourge of elfdom, causing the tiniest heart to palpitate in fear, releasing the shudder, twizzling the toes, while shivering and pickling the gizzard--a malady so intense the eyes redden and bulge in abstract horror---Tallitis; a seven-week disease leaving the once- proudly minuscule elf with swollen hands, feet, nose, ears, arms, and legs, while skyrocketing the victim to an incredible, freakish FOUR FEET IN HEIGHT! Saints be praised, mothers kiss your babies, eat a bowl of four leaf clovers, bolt the doors, hide in the bomb shelter, buy a rabbit's foot, cross all your fingers if you're double jointed, and HOPE FOR THE BEST!

Elf Randy wasn't so lucky.

About a month ago, he had noticed his little toe wasn't dwarfed anymore. It had grown overnight and was challenging his big toe for Top Little Piggie. He tried to ignore it. He thought it was just a fluke and then, his left ear sprouted movement towards his neck-- terrifying. He had to wear a scarf and hat to disguise his "ear"-uption. Two days later, the nose became bulbous, the right knee, a mountain, and his lips ballooned to the size of inner tubes. There were not enough hats or scarves to disguise it anymore.

"You have TALLITIS!" screamed Elf Candy. She released one of those squeals common in the final scene of a horror picture show.

Well, everyone knew. Elf Randy was forced to live in the stable with the reindeer because no one was quite sure if Tallitis was contagious. Santa visited, seemingly immune, and the reindeer nuzzled Randy's expanding portions.

Randy drew up his will, the only decent and respectable thing for a billowing and bloating former gnome-with-no-home to do.

Will-drawing-up was easy. He had one possession--a pocket watch given to him by his grandfather. It sang-- *What's it all about, Elfie?* He loved it. He bequeathed it, in the event of his deceaseness or gross expansion, to Mandy. He guessed that meant he loved her. She would like the watch.

Meanwhile back at our ever-increasing tale, Randy busted out of his clothes and Mrs. Kringle had to darn him a robe, made out of a used blanket from a reindeer stall. Things were "looking up", but for an elf with Tallitis, that was bad.

Dr. Ulandi risked a visit. "I have been thinking about Tallitis," he said, scratching his beard.

"Do you have a cure?" Randy was desperate.

"If the problem is big, then we need to think small--yes, think small. I want to try something."

"Anything," pleaded Randy.

Dr. Ulandi pulled out a handful of pills. "What makes us shrink more than diet pills? Then I want you to soak in a bath tub of lemon juice, read a story by Edgar Allen Poe, drink seven cups of coffee . . ."

"Wait, I don't understand," interrupted Randy.

Dr. Ulandi heaved a sigh. "You see, diet pills make you lose weight, lemon juice causes you to shrivel and pucker, the story will cause you to shrink back in fear, and the coffee will stunt your growth."

"You think this will work?"

"No, but it will keep us occupied until you explode."

"Explode?"

"Just kidding. But anyway, the final step to my ingenious treatment is to dress you in a cotton nightshirt and throw you in the washer on the hot cycle."

"What?"

"It sure shrunk my pee-jamers last week." Ulandi twinkled with a smile while furrowing a stern brow, all at the same time.

Elf Randy agreed to try it. He followed each step, faithfully. Coffee breathed, shivering from fear, lemony, and well dieted, he dove in the washer. Round and round he went in the oversized contraption, an elf needing Cheering, swept by the Tide. When the cycle was finished Ulandi shouted, "Hurry, throw him in the hot dryer on 'whites only' cycle!"

It was done.

The dryer stopped tumbling.

The door was opened. Steam and damp elf smell swelled out into the room.

A leg plopped out the door--a tiny leg-- then another. Randy dropped to the floor, a new pixie--healed.

"It's a miracle!" he exclaimed.

Doctor Ulandi gasped, then regained his composure, proclaiming, "You are re-elfed."

Randy returned to shop life. A cure for Tallitis had been found. Dr. Ulandi submitted his findings to a medical journal. They declined to publish due to limited readership amongst tiny toymakers.

Ulandi summarized the day. "Well, as they say--it all comes out in the wash!"

DECEMBER 6

Kris, Kirsten and Katerina

Kris Kringle sat at the table gazing at the woman he loved. It was supper time at the North Pole compound--dinner for 33--elves in chairs at tiny tables cluttered with huge bowls of steaming food; a warm sensation--family.

She made it that way.

Her name is Katerina and she is the portal to his soul, the master key to his logic, the strength to his notion. He loves her. To the idle beholder she is not beautiful; rather, sturdy, wise, and free of the inhibition, which causes many a woman to appear frail and needy.

She is his Katerina--Mrs. Santa Claus.

He breathes deeply, recalling the moment they met. He was an emotional wreck. He had just lost his first wife, Kirsten.

Kirsten.

She had been thread to his needle as he strove to weave the fabric of his dream--toys for all the children of Amsterdam at Christmas time. He was a struggling carpenter and cobbler who spent every waking hour building toys, at times to the detriment of his daily business. Kirsten organized the shop, placed the orders, found the children to help, and plotted the most clever ways to deliver the toys. The sleigh was her idea, and the red garment so Kris would be easily seen on foggy Christmas Eves. She trained the first reindeer, Comet and Cupid (so named Comet for the height of their dreams and Cupid for the depth of their love.) She was magnificent, funny, kind . . .and about twenty pounds underweight, with an ashen-ivory complexion, forewarning fragility.

It was during the hottest Amsterdam summer ever; she fell ill with a fever.

She needed medicine.

There was none.

She needed ice to cool her body.

The ice wagons were depleted.

She died in his arms.

Kris swore never to be without ice again.

Life had ceased. Kris put an advertisement in the Amsterdam newspaper soliciting a "young man, good with woods and glue." To his surprise the advertisement was answered by a spunky lady, strong as the wind, who saw no reason why she couldn't do the work.

He hired her, they worked.

He trusted her, they prospered.

He cared for her, she sparkled.

He grew interested, they kissed.

He loved her, marriage.

Now here he was with his lovely lady, around a table of plenty, with small companions galore.

Santa's eyes and cheeks gleamed with tears.

Two elves cleared their throats, discontent to wait any longer for delicious grub.

Santa lifted his head to the ceiling and said, "Thanks."

Food was passed, biscuits buttered, and corn chomped.

Santa smiled at Katerina, who was sipping hot chocolate.

It was a good day at the shop.

DECEMBER 7

Blizz, the Christmas Walrus

He wandered into the North Pole compound one night during a particularly ferocious snowstorm--ten feet long, weighing 2000 pounds, frigid and frightened, with the most adorable set of whiskers ever wiggled. The elves named him Blizz because they found him in the middle of a blizzard. He was really cute in a gargantuan kind of way. And . . .he was far from home.

The elves decided they would adopt him. Santa questioned the plan. "He is welcome if he wants to stay, but remember, it is temporary."

Elf Brandy bubbled, "Won't it be nice to have someone around who is actually bigger than you?'

Santa frowned. "I don't think that is the issue," he growled.

Well, actually it did end up being the issue. Blizz tried to fit in. He was big, bigger than anything around. He attempted toy-making but ended up crushing all the toy cars and trucks. He tried to help in the kitchen, but the room was too small (though his tusks were helpful in opening cans.) It took ten elves, fishing everyday for shellfish, to keep him in eats.

The work was not getting done.

"What's wrong with you?' screamed Elf Brandy. "Why can't you fit in?"

"I am a walrus," explained Blizz.

"But if you want to stay you have to find some way to be more like us--elf-like."

Blizz squinted, causing his whiskers to flicker. " I am a walrus," he repeated.

All was not going well.

It was decided Blizz should be the night watchman, to protect the shop from intruders. (There had never been any visitors let alone intruders. Well, there was a hockey team from Iceland that wanted to train nearby. They changed their minds when they saw the flying reindeer.)

Blizz was a horrible security guard--fell asleep the first night. Everyone was so disappointed in him. Brandy demanded an explanation.

"I am a walrus," Blizz sighed.

Then something extraordinary happened. Twenty of the elves were sent to Icicle Point to retrieve a delivery of supplies. Blizz decided to accompany them so he wouldn't feel useless around the toyshop. Several of the elves rode on his back as others skated alongside. As they journeyed, Blizz noticed that some of the surroundings looked familiar--well, familiar to a walrus who can distinguish subtle nuances in landscapes of white. While the elves crossed the tundra to secure the supplies, Blizz decided to explore. He was so excited. It appeared he had found his herd--he was home sweet home.

Suddenly Blizz heard a wee cry--then two, three--a half dozen. He scurried towards the sounds. There in the distance--elf destruction. For you see, the supplies had been too heavy. Elves and crates were breaking through, all across the ice.

"Help!" came a unified scream from everywhere.

Blizz leaped into the air, dove and cracked the ice, swimming towards the helpless little drowners.

"Grab my tusks," he shouted, as he swam collecting his friends and their cargo.

Brandy gasped. "Look, it's Sandy. She has slid under the ice, way down there--how will we get her out--she's trapped!"

"Everybody hold your breath," Blizz instructed. He submerged, swam under the ice, Sandy grabbed a piece of tusk, and then with one huge thrust, Blizz used his head to shatter the ice, surfacing, splashing along until the whole kit and kabootle were secure on safer turf.

"Thank you," gasped Elf Sandy.

"How did you do that?" queried Brandy.

"It's what I do. I am a walrus, " Blizz said humbly.

All at once, as if they had heard it for the first time, the elves comprehended.

Blizz was a walrus--a great walrus.

He was not a misfit toy maker, or lousy night watchman.

He was a walrus and he was home.

There were hugs and whisker tugs. "I am so glad you came into my life," Blizz said, dribbling some tears. "I can't be an elf, but I can bring your Christmas spirit to my berg."

"And we can be more walrus-like," Mandy smiled. "Or am I treading on thin ice?"

She giggled and everybody threw snowballs at her.

The elves returned to their homes minus the walrus. Blizz was home and successful.

After all, he was a walrus.

Brandy knew Blizz was happy. Still, she would miss her TON OF FUN.

🎁 DECEMBER 8 🎁

Mr. Kringle's Attitude for Gratitude

Not every preparation for the Christmas season is filled with the same zest and zeal, at least not at North Pole, Inc. Elves and reindeers experience mood swings, not to mention Santa's occasional bouts with grumpiness. (Remember, for your own sake, don't mention it!)

Many theories have been advanced concerning the different attitudes which trouble the shop. Dr. Ulandi believed it to be a lacking in Vitamin J, the joy elixir for little folk and hooved beings. Elf Tandy advanced the theory that electronic waves generated by the new computer system (used to replace the Big List, which had broken into pieces having been checked once or twice too often) were the culprit. Then there was Elf Handy, who thought the elfin "sad sacks" was due to a lack of music with vitality and oompah, so he played marches over the stereo loud speakers until all the elves started to scurry about, banging into each other.

Still, there were seasons within the season lacking joyous Yuletide seasoning.

The elves arrived to work one day to discover a huge sign four times taller than an elf standing on his pointed-shoe toes. It was entitled IF--a lollipop 'I" with a candy cane "F". It read:

> If we will not complain
> And drive our friends insane
> Then we can start to learn
> A newer leaf we turn
> To discover who we are
> Will take us very far
> And knowing what we're not
> Will help us find our slot
> So we can face the bad
> With hope instead of sad
> And then receive the good
> With thanks, just like we should
> For today's the only teacher
> Of every living creature
> To make this statement true
> THERE IS NOTHING WE CAN'T DO!

> Love,
> Mr. Kringle

The elves stood and stared for a long time, transfixed by the poem before them. Then they turned and peered at one another, a few with misty eyes, knowing they could do better. A tiny chortle blossomed amongst them, which became a giggle, culminating in an uproarious laugh.

They all as one realized they had become too serious about what was meant to be joyful.

They worked that day in a hum of contented glee.

Life was simpler.

Life was good.

🎁 DECEMBER 9 🎁
Let There Be Snow

Long, long ago in a time fresh and new when long ago was not possible because the Universe had just begun, there was a meeting; a most prestigious conclave, held on the surface of the Moon, to discuss matters that perplex and befuddle gods and all of their Cohort Beings. Present were Skylar, the master caretaker of the heavens, and Eartha, the mothering spirit of a fledgling planetoid effort, presently distinguished by the numeration 63-WL--the sixth galaxy from the Numbrite Center, third planet, WL--with life.

Eartha and Skylar were old companions from their training days at the Holenius Tresteleeen; therefore the conversation was breezy--a bit of planets, a dribble of star configurations, and some moon dust and craters thrown in to reflect the surroundings.

Eartha changed the subject. "Now, as to why I called our meeting."

Skylar sat back, leaning his massive energy-being against a nearby mountain, crumbling the side, causing rocks to cascade to the surface. Eartha smirked.

Skylar sat up. "Sorry, don't know my own nebulous."

They shared a cosmic chortle.

Eartha continued. "I have a problem--perhaps a small one, yet still troublesome. I could use some intervention from the heavens."

Skylar bowed. "My Universe is your Universe."

Eartha blushed and continued, "It is about 63-WL."

"Oh yes, that one--trouble from the start. The whole atmosphere and water for life situation. I don't know why they don't abandon it . . ."

"A pet project," Eartha concluded.

"Give me one hundred comets any day," Skylar snorted, restoring some rocks to the mountain he had disrupted.

"Well, anyway," Eartha continued, "it's the whole ground thing."

"Ground?"

"Yes, the hazard of my trade, terra firma. Dirt *en mass*, if you will."

Skylar nodded, somewhat unfamiliar with the turf but willing to listen and learn.

Eartha explained. "What we have is cold mud and frozen grass."

Skylar shrugged. "I don't know. Is this bad?"

"Ugly, impractical, and messy, would be better stated. We do have rain."

"Rain?" Skylar squinted.

"Water from the sky. Our dear friend Wind stirs the atmosphere to form clouds . . ."

Skylar had sprouted a full face of confusion.

Eartha saw his dilemma and inserted, "Well, back to the problem."

"Messy mud and gooey grass."

"Precisely!"

"What's wrong with that?"

Eartha gasped, releasing a cloud of dust. "Well, besides being ugly, it is difficult for creatures to move about, and it doesn't keep things cold enough to maintain winter life or warm enough to welcome the heat-absorbing creatures."

"So, what is it you want from me?" queried Skylar, with that characteristic practicality and directness common to those of the celestial.

Eartha paused. "I don't know. I guess I need a rain that doesn't make mud but stays around long enough to keep things cold while beautiful enough to make things crystalline."

Skylar grunted. "Well, this is a predicament suitable for a master of the heavens."

"That is why I came to you," Eartha fawned.

"Let me see. Let's start with some water."

"We have that," Eartha interrupted.

"You have dribbles and dabs. I have The Big Dipper at my disposal, filled with wonderful wet."

Eartha bowed her bead, bettered.

"But what good is water without some new approach?" Skylar contemplated as Eartha mused. Suddenly he sat straight up, causing the Moon to shift, sliding half of it into darkness. "I have it."

"Tell me, tell me," Eartha exploded.

"I will take one of the stars from my constellations, one burned out and cold, and drop it in my Big Dipper until the water freezes solid."

Eartha was fully attentive and grounded into the explanation.

Skylar continued, "Then I will take the hind legs of my *Canis Major* to dig at the surface of the frozen Big Dipper until flakes and fluff fly everywhere in the air, tumbling through frigid galaxies towards 63-WL."

"Flakes and fluff . . ." Eartha repeated.

"Then you must get Wind to blow the units about until they land and pile up in white clumps of beautiful mountains--slippery and wet but cold and solid."

Eartha wept. "What a beautiful idea. Do you think it will work?"

"All things are accomplished when Skylar and Eartha are at one together."

"I don't know how to thank you," Eartha gushed.

" Well, let me name this concoction. Let's see we start with a star--S--then I will add an N--for the cooperation of the Nebula. An O--for its journey through Orion and a W, yes, a W for the work of our dear friend, Wind. S-N-O-W."

"Snow!" Eartha pronounced with a holy regality.

"LET THERE BE SNOW!!" Skylar bellowed.

. . . and there was snow--to cover the messy mud and gooey grass, cool the planet, while making homes for all things winter. And . . . IT WAS GOOD!

DECEMBER 10

Happy Birthday, Mr. Kringle

Everybody is born. So with Kris Kringle, birthed in 1623, of peasant parents who were charged and commissioned by the city fathers to clean the streets of Amsterdam--wage, food and shelter. There was never extra but always seemed to be enough to relieve the ache of hunger and a roof to protect from the chill. Kris learned to scrounge and repair. His mother and father brought home bits and pieces of once whole objects, which he carved, whittled and glued until a toy emerged from the rubble.

There was no school, so he was befriended by a kindly parson who took a liking to him, gave him scraps, and taught him to read and cipher.

His parents died when he was twelve, crushed by a carriage rumbling along the streets late at night. The Parson, Nicolas VanEeves, took him in and let him clean the church and do repairs for a meal a day and a straw mattress in the bell tower. Kris was surrounded by candles, prayers, bells and music. Fearing bats in the tower, he learned to sleep lightly and arise early to avoid their company.

One of the congregation members of the church, a successful businessman, took him in as an apprentice at his cabinet shop. Kris learned the craft of woods, nails, epoxy, paints and varnishes. In no time he was head master of his department, yearning for more challenge.

His heart dwelled with the children. A jubilant spirit and an explosive laugh caused the little ones to follow him everywhere--the Pied Piper of Amsterdam.

His greatest passion was crafting toys. Every year he would make a list of the children he wanted to bless with a Christmas gift, then he would take each available waking moment to work on their projects, careful not to shirk his duties. He never wanted the children to know they came from him so he would attach a note on each gift: FROM ST. NICOLAS, thus honoring the parson, his longtime benefactor,

The children of Amsterdam began to wish and dream of gifts from St. Nick, as they called him. Kris prospered and started his own little shop, marrying Katerina when he was 27 years old. They spent the next thirty or more years, loving, working, and giving toys from St. Nicolas.

Then on Kris Kringle's sixtieth birthday, December 10, 1683, he received a visit. 'Twas a cold, icy night.

Kris was busy at his bench, working on another wooden horse for a little boy named Enoch. There was a rap on the door. Kris opened it and there, hunched over, was a very short man, adorned in rags, dripping with ice and snow, shivering. Kris ushered him in and sat him by the fire. The tiny gentleman removed the scarf from his head, unveiling a countenance--grotesque and twisted; bulging warts on his nose and his skin was pocked, wrinkled and darkened, like a charred piece of firewood.

Kris cringed. "Are you well, my brother?" The question seemed appropriate, given the spectacle before him.

"Not as well as you, Kris Kringle." His voice was smooth and low, a sharp contrast from his ghastly appearance.

"You know my name?"

"I know your deeds."

"Then perhaps I should bow my head. My deeds are peppered with mistakes."

"Your deeds are filled with love."

Kris peered at the curious little fellow. "Have you shelter?"

"Now I do."

Kris prepared some soup and a bit of tea. He fed the man and found an old cloak to warm him. "I am afraid the garment is moth eaten, but still removes a chill or two." Kris patted his shoulder.

"Kris Kringle, you will never taste of death until time has exhausted herself."

"And what might you mean, kind sir?"

"I am the very least and you have done it."

"Done what?"

"Details distract us from our work."

"Is there more I can do for you, pilgrim?"

"I have come to do for you." The stranger opened his threadbare coat, revealing a gorgeous snow globe. "This is your new home."

Kris peered in at the ornate cottage surrounded by snow. "I think I will need a bit larger. I am a man of girth and this is small," he chuckled.

"Faith is always birthed in small vessels. Please listen to me--at a time of your heart's desire you and Katerina can place this globe in your hands, close your eyes, whisper, 'My hour is come' and you will be transported to this cottage--a beautiful palace of ice and snow where you may build toys for the children of the world."

"Such a dream," Kris said with tears in his eyes, "but I am old, not trusting the fantasy of strangers."

"Then trust this." The tiny fellow held the globe aloft. It glistened and gleamed, firing a burst of light and an explosion of energy into the very soul of the aging toy maker.

"Saints be praised!" shouted Kris, gasping for air. "Are you a sorcerer?"

The man continued. "You will age only one year in a hundred, to be celebrated on this tenth day of December."

"Only one year older every hundred years. It is a fantasy. Such good deeds could be done with that blessing of time."

"And they shall."

These were the closing words of the visitor. In a wisp of a moment, he swirled into a great cone of smoke and gleam, changing into a golden snow, which trickled and fell into the iridescent globe.

He was gone.

For two months Kris kept the visit a secret. He finished delivery of his "St. Nick" toys and continued about his business.

Then something utterly evil and bizarre transpired. A group of concerned citizens pandered a petition asking the magistrate to outlaw the giving of toys at Christmas because it was "an intrusion into people's homes" and "unfair to the youngsters who did not receive."

Amazingly, the law was passed. Toy making was fine. Distribution of toys was forbidden.

Toys would have to be sold in the stores.

Kris and Katerina believed their work in Amsterdam was finished. Kris shared with his wife the strange "vision" of December 10th. She smiled, wondering if too much time with the glues had left him dazed, but she agreed such a place would be lovely.

On February 10th, 1684, Kris and Katerina placed the globe between them and in one voice repeated, "My hour is now come."

A whirl and a chill in a dizzying second they found themselves in a huge workshop surrounded by little folk, smiling, giggling, and culminating with a cheer. "Welcome, Mr. Kringle," said one of the minuscule ones.

"Where am I?" They both spoke in wonder as one.

"Home. It is December 10th, your 61st birthday and you better enjoy it because you won't have another one for a hundred years."

They laughed. Food was provided, music played, and dances danced with the glee of souls sanctified.

Kris was truly home.

Happy Birthday, Mr. Kringle!

✠ DECEMBER 11 ✲

The Unstable Thief

Philip despised crowds--loud, boisterous, confining, and smelly. He hated the sense of being surrounded and swallowed up, losing all space and identity to a common horde. Yet, large gatherings of people were the hazard of his profession--the factors of his trade. Without crowds there are no people, without people there are no possessions, and without possessions, well, there is no occupation for him.

Philip is a thief; a good one. Of course, not good in the sense of morality. Philip acknowledges his thievery as a character flaw, an unfortunate choice he has made due to the hard times. He tried to be a laborer but was weak, dismissed by countless employers. He tried farming but nothing grew. He even joined the army. He lacked the stamina for the marches. He considered all of his options and decided stealing was the least offensive to his gentle consciousness. He did have standards, set by himself, which he had dubbed "The Big Three":

1. Never steal from women or children or souls less wealthy than himself.

2. Never do bodily harm to another

3. Give one dollar of every ten to the poor
It was a simple justification, from a simple man.

He had come to town because of the crowds. Crowds made it easier to steal. Sometimes people would lay their pouches down for a moment, resting. It was easily snatched. People pressed together have their belongings lifted by nimble fingers. Sometimes money just fell out on the ground. There were many ways to relieve the rich of their cumbersome purses.

It had been a good day--two moneybags, a necklace, three golden goblets, and a silver medallion. Philip was always relieved when he could take his haul and escape. He had never been caught. There had been a few close calls, but he was always able to talk himself out of a nasty predicament--until this evening.

He was being followed. He had taken a chance on stealing the medallion. The merchant was asleep and it dangled from his neck like a succulent clump of wild grapes. Philip was careful, but slow. One of the guards saw him; at least Philip thought he did. Philip made a hasty retreat, but there was that gnawing sensation that he was being trailed. Was it the guard? Would a hired agent be that persistent?

It made him nervous. He hated the sensation of being stalked.

Then . . . "Chilly night?" The voice appeared out of nowhere, basal and raspy.

Philip jerked around. It was the guard. "Yes," he replied breathing deeply.

"Are you from town?"

"No, out of town." What a stupid answer. Did the guard recognize him? Did he hear the tension in Philip's voice?

"I saw you today."

Philip froze, waiting.

"Was that your friend with the medallion?"

"Medallion?"

"Were you taking it to have it polished?'

The guard knew. Philip was terrified. Thievery was punishable by death--on the spot. He didn't know what to do. He ran. He ran and ran until his wheezing breath blocked out all sound. He stopped long enough to stash his treasures in a nearby alley. He would have to retrieve them later. He could still hear the shuffling of feet from behind. He ran, finally ducking into an Inn, so crowded he had to descend the stairs to the stable.

It stunk.

How he hated stink, animal stink the worst. He dove into the hay finding refuge behind two sheep and an ox. He lay there, sweating, panting, sucking in large breaths of the putrid air, feeling achy and nauseous. He listened--nothing. Had he escaped the guard? He listened again. A sheep nuzzled his cheek. He swatted it away. He was exhausted. He lay quietly in the damp, moldy straw, motionless, until sleep overcame him. All at once, there was a rustle on the steps. Philip jerked to attention. There were voices, two--men. He had been discovered. The guard would recognize him.

Then a notion came to his head--a brilliant plan. He removed all of his cloths and threw them over a contented lamb. He wrapped himself in a discarded piece of homespun cloth, apparently used for one of the animals. He drew the garment up over his head, covering his face. He stood to his feet and shouted, "Be careful, leper. Leper!" He walked towards the stairs.

"What are you doing done there?" came the voice from above.

It didn't sound like the guard, but Philip knew he must be cautious.

"I was cold, and didn't think my disease would harm the creatures."

"Well, it will these creatures."

"We are sorry to disturb you, pilgrim." It was a woman's voice--soft, weak, and low.

Philip was relieved. "No, let me by and I will be gone." He climbed the stairs, aware of three beings in the darkness. They stood to the side, silently. Once he was to the entrance, he opened the door and scurried into the night. He decided to keep his leper garb, just in case he ran into the tenacious guard.

He was done with this town, deciding to take his prizes and leave. He wondered if he should sneak back to the stable and retrieve his clothes. Then he remembered the woman and the souls on the stairs. What were they doing there? Were they staying? It was too risky. He would have plenty of money to buy a new robe and cloak.

Maybe his clothes would keep the lamb warm.

They were old and tattered anyway. He trodded on--a thief without garments, feverishly on the run.

****

And Mary bore her first son, Jesus, wrapping him in *swaddling clothes* she found, cast aside, nearby, and laid him in a stable.

DECEMBER 12

North Pole Stew

You boil some ice
Until it's nice
And add a cup
Of wild grain rice.

And if you want to share it
Add two cups of diced-up carrot.
Watch the fire, don't burn it up
But add right in three-sliced turnip.

It isn't time to take a seat
Add a pound of fresh meat.
And if you really want to please
Add a cup of shredded cheese.

Take an onion and don't ask why
Cut it up, please don't cry
Potatoes are nice
Or just more rice
A hint of garlic
And pepper, we said
Not the Doctor, green or red.

Take stalk of yourself
With celery you know

A half a cup
And watch it grow.

Stir in some broth from chicken
If the stew you want to quicken
Then add a beet to make it sweet
And some corn will help adorn
Your glorious bubbling treat.

With color and taste
Don't spill or waste
Stir for an hour
If you've got the power,
On a low fire
And soon you'll require . . .

Six fine bowls to serve it up
Or some may prefer a smaller cup
And top it off with sour cream
You will have a cooker's dream.

Yes, be so proud when you are through
You have made NORTH POLE STEW.

⊞ DECEMBER 13 ⛟
Daviatha

Daviatha was in trouble, a planet poised for destruction: a casualty of an irrevocable, natural disaster. Its sun had begun to implode causing the daytime temperatures to soar to blistering, scorching heights, while the night hours became a frigid tomb of chilling frost and ice. Nature was in disarray. The animals were hostile, coming to the cities for shelter-- snarling, attacking and biting. The waters froze and steamed all within the same day, squelching all sea life.

It was just a matter of time. How long would depend on what expert you spoke to on any given day. Yet, none thought there would be more than a *wizzled drepe*--12 days.

Morish was the first one awake. There was little use for sleep. The house was either an oven or an iceberg. It did still provide shelter from burns and frostbite. He was a successful businessman, silver export. Successful? The word seemed without definition. Perhaps success now would be an extra hour or *wizzle*. Silver lacked promise--gleam-less.

Morish was married to a delightful, intelligent musician, Jera. She was the vibrant epicenter of their eruptive life. An only son, Teran, was bright, articulate, and athletic--a promising child, now engulfed, with them, in a doom-watch.

Tears were frequent with gasps of anxiety and fits of rage. All useless.

The sun would implode, the planet burst into flames.

They would die.

Morish contemplated. How should you spend the last moments of your life?

"Couldn't sleep?" came the soft voice from the door. It was Jera, standing in the candlelight, a silhouetted beauty.

"No," Morish replied, moving her way.

"Me, either." Teran stumbled in and joined them in the meager light.

"It seems wasteful to sleep," Jera chuckled.

Morish smiled. Wasteful? What an insightful, accurate word.

Teran hugged his dad. "I am having nightmares."

"I would be shocked if you weren't, but if you don't mind, let us not share dark dreams and squander our precious time."

Jera nodded and Teran sniffed, wiping his eyes of determined tears.

"Will it hurt?" Teran asked.

"No," replied Morish.

"Like a deep breath of heat, a flash of light--over." Jera was somber, but gentle.

Morish marveled at her explanation, comforted. Had she thought of this earlier or was it a moment of inspiration?

"Something to eat?" Jera inquired.

Both males shook their heads--not hungry.

They sat in silence--an occasional mournful siren in the distance, but no chirping, or barking, or other sounds at all.

Life was dying before the dying hour.

"I hope it means something," Teran said quietly.

"What?' Jera asked, stroking his hair.

Morish interrupted. "Our planet's death-- our death, am I right? That's what you mean."

"Right, Dad. How did you know?"

"You stole my thoughts."

"And mine," whispered Jera.

"Well, if we all have the question, who will answer?" Teran grumbled.

"There are only thoughts and hopes. Answers are not in our reach," Morish said.

"I think death brings life, otherwise, why the fuss?" Jera softened the conversation. She was music--metered, harmonious, and melodic to all who would hear.

Morish swallowed hard. "It must have a reason. God knows, I must believe there is a reason for so much destruction and death."

"I, too." Jera kissed her husband's head.

"Count me in," Teran exclaimed, cuddling in to complete the threesome.

It was at that moment the sun gave up its life struggle. An explosion, never before known; heat, fire, gases, a tremendous flash of light swept across the planet once known as Daviatha, swallowing all form and life, squelching the breath and soul from all moving creatures, searing and molding them into a gigantic glowing mass of gelatinous matter, propelling across the Universe, absorbing solar system after galaxy--a horrific wonder of such magnitude that all Eternity watched with an awful disbelief.

Life on Daviatha was over, but its incandescence zoomed through the blackened night--thousands of years of travel--light begetting light.

* * * * * * * * * * * * *

Four men dressed in woolen robes, gnawed their bread and sipped some wine and headed for a field filled with animals--sheep. As they gazed into the night, their eyes were bedazzled by a glorious, shimmering glow. "Star of David!" they exclaimed.

* * * * * * * * * * * * * *

In the cavernous halls of a monarch's castle, six souls stare into the heavens at a spectacular visage. They are kings and rulers-- stargazers from the East near the Great Mountains. "Star of Divinity," Santere, their leader, proclaims.

* * * * * * * * * * * * * *

Splitting the night sky with a brilliant glimmer of the vestige of a once great people-- across millions of miles and thousands of years- -it was a star.

Morish, Jera and Teran's essence.
THE STAR OF DAVIATHA!

✠ DECEMBER 14 ✱

All The Reindeer Games

When you have too much time on your hooves, haunted by antler envy and Jack Frost nipping at your nose as young bucks-in-waiting are nipping at your heels for your job--well--it's enough to make any fine reindeer just a little grumpy. By December 14th all the reindeer team are picking at hairs (which can be quite painful if you only own one coat) You see, it's the whole "waiting for Santa, Christmas Eve and have I put on too much weight so I won't fly?" syndrome. Pretty soon you're bickering at bunkmates 'cause they got barley breath.

You see, at one time the elves held a competition called (appropriately) THE REINDEER GAMES, which was played to relieve some boredom, pressure, and to help keep the peace. It was a five-event contest:

1. Best rack of antlers
2. Finest grooming (comically referred to by the elves as "Smell and Tell")
3. Fastest one in the harness
4. Congeniality (big teeth a plus) and
5. THE RACE (first one to the North Pole and back!)

Well, the Reindeer Games had been stopped many years ago, mainly because the elves were tired of the continual schmoozing by the contestants (finding apples and hay on their pillows at night), cheating by the participants (once Comet duct-taped a defoliated bush to his head in an attempt to win Best Antlers) and of course, the whole discrimination suit by Rudolph and his family brought against the herd.

After the games were stopped things got worse. By Christmas Eve the herd was always disgruntled, reluctant, backbiting, and constipated from erratic eating habits and spastic colons.

Something had to be done.

Santa created an ice rink. Yes, an ice rink. He decided to have one REINDEER GAME-- a race. Ten times around the ice rink, last deer standing the winner. No one knows what possessed Santa--everyone knows reindeer have slippery hooves, and nothing could be more slippery than ice. Still . . . the race was held.

Santa was there, wearing ice skates and a pillow attached to his backside, which was most advantageous considering the number of times he slipped and bounced on the cushion. Santa whistled and regaled, "May the best reindeer win!"

Well . . . they were off. Comet went out front, slipped and tripped. Vixen sprawled forward, knocking over Cupid, who tumbled head over back legs into Donner, who single-handedly caboosed Rudolph and Blitzen. The next half hour was spent with reindeer trying to stand, only to plop into configurations and splits unnatural to their species. Elves held giggles as Santa looked on in horror. Rudolph made it around once before bottom sliding into a snow bank, leaving him buried. Dasher never made it out of the gate, Prancer's antlers stuck in the ice, and Dancer, well, didn't.

Valiantly they tried, skidding on bottoms and faces into each other and the snow.

After what seemed to be an eternity of daredevil collisions and painful squeals, Santa shouted, "For the love of God, STOP!"

The bruised and beaten contestants attempted to comply in mid-slide.

Bandages were supplied with extra doses of liniment for all.

That, my dear souls, was the last time the Reindeer games were brought up. From then on the gang favored Parcheesi.

Elf Grandy summed up the day best: "Reindeer can't skate."

The only good thing was, that with all the slipping and sliding and landing on their faces, no one would ridicule Rudolph ever again.

The whole herd was red-nosed!

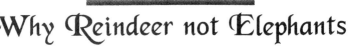

DECEMBER 15

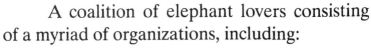

Why Reindeer not Elephants

A coalition of elephant lovers consisting of a myriad of organizations, including:

The Peanut Growers of North America

The Gray Panthers

Floppy Ears not Discs

Pachyderm Firm

Circus in a Trunk

Never Forget Inc.

Rhinoplasty.Org and

Tuskaterrific,

joined forces to send a petition to Mr. Kringle, surnamed Santa Claus, citing favoritism to reindeer in discrimination of the elephant. It read as follows:

Dear Mr. Claus:

How many children have ever seen a reindeer? I dare say, few. On the other hand, millions of them have enjoyed the elephant. He is adorable, functional, not to mention conversational and comedic. (How do you know if an elephant has been in your bathroom? You can still smell his peanut after-shave)

What would a circus be without an elephant? He is commercial. Note Disney's success with Dumbo--also a flying elephant.

Wouldn't the children love to tickle and rub their fuzzy jowls?

Why do you continue to overlook the elephant as a means of transportation? Dasher and Dancer may be great names but think of these--♫ You know Trunky and Grayling and Earsey and Tusky—Ton-sey and Funsy and Noser and Chunky ♫ Isn't this adorable?

In conclusion, we desire you reconsider your stance on the Great Gray Guy.

For your next Christmas JAUNT don't forget the Ele-PHANT!

Sincerely working for peanuts,

E. Corp

After several weeks, a communiqué was released from the Toyshop Press Corps. It read:

Dear E. Corp,

We love elephants.

We do not wish to ignore them. Presently reindeer are the preference of our CEO. He cites the following reasons:

1. He doesn't think his traveling companions should dwarf him.
2. A fear of Elf toe-jam from frolicking pachyderms.

3. Roof breakage on frequent landings.
4. No antlers.
5. Floppy ears create wind resistance
6. Gray clashes with red and green.
7. No peanuts for miles around.
8. No elephants for miles around.
9. Tusks repulse children.
10. Mrs. Kringle's recurring dream about wrinkled trunks swallowing Santa in the Hackensack Tunnel.

E. Corp continues their vigil. Who knows, someday we may look into the sky and see a sleigh pulled by two reindeer, two giraffe, two yaks, and of course--two elephants.

It worked for Noah and the Ark, why not the Claus?

DECEMBER 16

Santa's Prep For Pep

Elf Randy found a crumpled piece of paper in the trash. He unfolded it and read:

Santa's Prep for Pep

1.   Get up early. Don't keep the sun waiting or it will grow lonely on the job and start complaining about the long hours.

2.   Clean up until you know that you wouldn't mind sitting next to yourself.

3.   Put on just enough "smell good" so people can sniff you going, not coming.

4.   Before you eat, kiss somebody you love.

5.   Eat just enough to get you going--not so much that you find yourself staying.

6.   Say good morning to something that can't talk back.

7.   Take a moment to tell Life how grateful you are to still be moving.

8.   Start your day with a job you can do, quickly and well, so your heart will feel better about the tougher ones ahead.

9.   Take something to drink, it helps you think.

10.   Don't work with others until you are ready to forgive mistakes.

11.   Never eat and run. Enjoy the eat, take a breath, then do the run.

12.   Every ten minutes think something funny. Laugh. Someone will ask.

13.   Make something before you finish your day.

14.   Set a time limit not a goal. It's better for the soul.

15.   Tell a friend you were thinking about them.

16.   Life is fast. Have fun.

17. Finish the day with an easy task to reward your heart for staying faithful.

18. Make sure everyone you meet knows you wish them well.

19. Dine with friends and talk.

20. Ask God to watch over your night.

Randy smiled. He had taken a precious glimpse into the heart of his boss and friend.

DECEMBER 17
The Rugaboot

Elf Andy had a good idea. No, it was a great idea--an inspiration--the next best thing to striped candy canes. He could barely keep it to himself. He had been working on it for weeks, often sacrificing his other duties. He was thrilled. He could barely wait till the next SHOP TALK.

Once a week Santa would sit down with all the elves and have a community meeting where complaints could be heard and new ideas aired. Andy had a project and he was working very hard to get it done before the meeting. There were still a few bugs to be worked out but it certainly seemed ready for a test run.

Shop Talk night arrived. Andy was so excited he couldn't eat dinner. He sat quietly as several elves grumbled about porridge texture and mattress lumps. Finally, Santa opened the floor to suggestions. It was at that point Andy ran over to his invention, jumped inside, turned the ignition and zoomed through the room, crashing into three elves, two bicycles, and a huge box of candy; an accident hurling chocolate through the air and Elf Handy stuck in the spokes of a bicycle wheel.

"What's going on?" Santa demanded.

Elf Andy emerged from the wreckage, smeared with marshmallow and peanut better, red-faced, embarrassed. "It still has some wrinkles," he explained.

"Wrinkles? I think Elf Handy is the one who may be permanently wrinkled." Santa pointed towards the helpless elf, dangling in the air. Two buddies helped him down to safety.

"I'm sorry, Mr. Kringle. I was just so excited about my new invention," Andy said.

"Invention? It looks like a boot."

"It is," Andy proclaimed proudly.

"I don't want to hurt your feelings, Andy, but you didn't invent the boot. It has been around for centuries."

"No Santa. It's not just a boot. Behold-- THE RUGABOOT."

Santa crinkled his brow, confused. Elf Andy continued. "A great new toy to give to the children--a small pump that propels it along. And here is the cool part--it runs on water for fuel."

"But what is 'it'?"

"It is---THE RUGABOOT!"

"I know the name, but what does it do?"

"Speeds across the carpet--get it--a boot that races across the rug, thus, I dubbed it-- RUGABOOT."

Santa rolled his eyes. "I return to my question, what does it do, besides maim elves and crush chocolate bon-bons?"

The other elves giggled. Andy gave flitting glances of disgust and despair toward his mocking comrades. This was a disaster. The King of Toys did not understand his vision. "It moves fast, runs on water, and is . . . well, fun." Andy was nearly in tears.

"It's a boot," Santa punctuated.

"A RUGABOOT!"

"Andy, no matter how many ways you say it--it's still a boot. What child wants a boot?"

"Perhaps a shoeless one," Elf Grandy presented, trying to help, but causing the whole room to burst into laughter.

Elf Andy was offended. He pouted, protruding a lower lip that could have carried a pail of milk.

Santa stepped in to cease the ridicule. "I'm sorry, Andy. I don't mean to make fun, but it's a boot, and most children don't like their toys to come in footwear."

Andy was devastated. The meeting was dismissed. He went to his bed and tried to sleep, tossing and turning. When he finally did get to sleep, he had nightmares of Santa's shoe stepping on his head.

Days passed. Andy just couldn't seem to get over the fiasco at the SHOP TALK. Most of the elves tried to be kind, but some teased him. "Hey, Andy come over here and show me what's this all A-BOOT?" they would chide and giggle. He tried to be brave, but hurt is hurt and sometimes hurt just won't go away.

Then it happened. He should have known better. He should have asked for help. But he thought he could get it by himself. Santa climbed up on two empty crates, trying to get a jar of glue. The top crate broke and he came crashing to the floor, twisting his ankle.

"Do we have any ice?" Dr. Ulandi squealed.

"It's the North Pole, of course we have ice," Elf Grandy griped.

Ice was chopped and placed on the swollen ankle of the corpulent Claus. Two days passed, and it was no better. How could Santa deliver the toys with a tender, sore foot? Truly, he could ride in the sleigh, but when the sleigh landed, and he slid down the chimney, how could he move around each and every house delivering and displaying the gifts?

Then Elf Andy had another great idea. "Santa, why don't you use the RUGABOOT?"

"What do you mean?" Santa queried.

"I will make two RUGABOOTS to fit your feet, then you can scoot along the carpet and do your job so Christmas won't be canceled."

And so it was.

Andy made the boots, Santa practiced using them, toys were delivered and Christmas was saved. Andy was a hero--a genius. His invention wasn't just a toy. It was the SAVER of TOYS.

Andy beamed. "I got to dream and build a toy that gave Christmas to all the girls and boys."

In addition, Elf Andy was commissioned by a local hospital to build thirty pairs of RUGABOOTS for the children who could not walk, so they could zoom through the ward and play.

It was a champion of a day.

Santa was pleased.

Needless to say, Andy was praised and promoted.

But most important to Elf Andy--he didn't get THE BOOT.

✚ DECEMBER 18 🎁

ꙩhe ꙥegend of Ꙥonner and ꙥlitzen

The Vandertulips loved reindeer. Hans and Helga once owned a small herd, about ten, before the famine in the Lowlands forced them to sell them to gain substance for body and soul. There were two of the "dears" left--Noya and Foya--more pets than livestock.

The hard times persisted.

Soon there was no food for nourishment nor wood or coal for warmth; the winter cold, unusually harsh. The Vandertulips had moved the reindeer inside the house, trying to keep all of them warm. But soon hunger overtook them. Unfortunately, these last two reindeer were undernourished and would not glean any price at market. Hans and Helga anguished over the situation. They must live. So they decided to destroy their pet reindeer so they would have meat to eat, a horrible feeling. Yet, they had begged and borrowed and would not steal. Hans grabbed his musket with two remaining loads of shot and headed to the woods with Noya. He wept, lamented, argued with himself, and fretted. He looked over at Noya, who seemed forlorn and downcast. Did the beast know what he was going to do? He stopped at two farms trying to sell his companion. No one had money or food.

He trudged onward, further into the frigid forest. The snow grew deeper, making it difficult to move. He stopped next to a huge evergreen and prepared his musket. The barrel was tarnished and the flintlock was rusty. He loaded the powder, raised the gun towards Noya, closed his eyes . . .when suddenly there was the sound of tinkling bells. Hans opened one eye--saw nothing. Then he opened the other. There appeared a sleigh, pulled by two reindeer.

"Out hunting, my brother?" asked the personable young man in the long beard and hat.

"No," responded Hans, gazing at his musket.

"Well, I was going to say, you might not want to fire that gun."

"Why?"

"The barrel is bent. It will blow up in your hands--a nasty kick--might even kill you."

Hans peered at his weapon, his eyes filling with tears.

"What's wrong?' asked the young man as he climbed down from his sleigh.

"I can't even do bad, good," Hans cried.

"Listen, come over here in the sleigh and tell me about it. My name is Kris, Kris Kringle."

"I'm Hans Vandertulip and I was trying to shoot my reindeer."

Kris lurched back in disbelief. "Why would you want to kill such a fine animal?"

Noya snorted in appreciation to the compliment.

"I don't. We are hungry. They are all we have to eat." Hans fell into a puddle of tears.

Kris patted the man's shoulder, gazing over at the reindeer. "You say 'they'. Are there more?"

"One more. This is Noya and Foya is at home, awaiting her fate."

"This is not good," mused Kris, rubbing his beard. "These are pets and friends, not food."

"I know that. Don't you think I have tried everything?" Hans pleaded.

Kris sat for a long moment while the winds of twilight whistled and whinnied past his ears. At length he spoke. "Let me give you some bacon and flour I have in the sleigh. You give me Noya and your musket. I will fix your musket and meet you back here at noon tomorrow. You bring Foya and we will make plans."

Hans agreed--anything to keep from murdering his antlered friend.

True to his word, Kris met Hans the next day. Hans was standing there holding the reins to Foya.

Kris spoke. "Listen, I have been thinking. I have a surprise. I fixed your musket and brought you some shot. I also took the liberty to make this for you." Kris held up a magnificent bow with a quiver of nine arrows.

"This is for me?" gasped Hans.

"With the musket and the bow you should be able to hunt for food in these woods."

"You are a good man, Kris Kringle."

"I can't let you starve and certainly won't stand by and watch the slaughter of two excellent reindeer."

"How can I thank you?" Hans pumped Kris' hand as if anticipating a spurting of water.

Kris gently pulled away and said, "Let me care for Noya and Foya until you are well and strong again. I will love them as my own."

Hans agreed, marching away, alternating between lifting his bow and shaking his musket.

Kris took Noya and Foya and welcomed them as family into his home. Comet and Cupid accepted them into the barn and all was well. Noya and Foya ate and ate, regaining their plumpness and preen.

When spring came Kris took them out into the community, trying to return the well-fattened creatures to Hans. Hans was nowhere to be found. Not a soul knew of his whereabouts.

Kris took the pair back to his abode. "Well, I guess you are stuck with me."

The duo leaped and nuzzled the young man.

"I do not like your names. If you don't mind I have a desire to change them. Foya because you have recovered quite well and it seems you DON a whole new countenance and vitality, I shall call you DONNER. And you, Noya, because you escaped death like a BLITZ in the nick of time, you should definitely be dubbed BLITZEN.

The reindeer smiled, if that is what they do.

So two creatures headed for slaughter were saved by a craftsman named Kris Kringle.

And now you know how Santa got his Donner and his Blitzen.

DECEMBER 19

Kris' Tires

One of the more difficult jobs at Toyshop Central is the whole "GOING TO FIND OUT WHO'S NAUGHTY AND NICE" dilemma. First of all, no one wants to go around being critical and picky. Secondly, it is really not very friendly to snitch. And finally, THE LIST upkeep and checking it twice can give you back aches and eyestrain.

Special elves were needed, ones who balanced each other's personalities. Elf Grandy was selected because he was critical, although he preferred the word analytical. Elf Mandy was chosen for her compassion and soft, gooey heart, counteracting Grandy's, "ana-critical" nature. Elf Tandy was chosen because he was good with computers and figures and Elf Dandy was selected because well . . . he knew how to fly.

That brings me to the story.

In days of old the job of evaluating the children's behavior was easier. The elves received letters and each boy and girl would share what their year had been like.

"I was good"

"I was bad on October 23rd"

"I helped Mommy"

"I disobeyed Daddy"

Simple.

Then children started watching politicians speak on TV. They learned how to "package their presentation."

"I am better than my sister"

"I have seen worse'

"It wasn't my fault"

"The devil made me do it"

"Considering the circumstances, it was the best I could do"

"It all depends what you mean by 'naughty' and 'nice' "

The Elf committee would have to go check it out onsite. Public transportation was out--too big, too weird, they too well known.

To make a long story short, Santa bought a hot-air balloon.

It was on sale from a tire company--big. Emblazoned on the side was *Fineday Tires.* The company requested their name be removed. The elves thought a balloon might be less conspicuous if it had some advertising so they painted over *Fineday*, and wrote *Kris'* above *Tires.*

They all thought it was a hoot. Elves are like that.

Preparations were made, the balloon was filled, and the elves were "up, up and away". The trip was successful. No one suspected anything, certainly not a balloon carrying emissaries from the North Pole, spying on the behavioral patterns of little children. The elves took turns standing on each other's shoulders so they could see over the basket and into the world beyond.

It was a successful trip until . . . they came across a near-sighted duck, apparently lost, on his way south. He couldn't see where he was going, slammed into the side, bounced off, but his bill poked a hole in the side of the balloon.

The duck was fine. The balloon wasn't.

Air was pouring out of the side and the "elves-in-a-basket" began to descend. They were somewhere over Siberia.

"I don't want to be captured by the commies," Elf Grandy squealed.

"They are not commies anymore. They are our friends and allies," Mandy corrected.

Friend or foe, the balloon was about to go.

"We need to fill that hole," said Elf Tandy, blessed with a gift for the obvious.

They thought and thought, all the time getting lower and lower.

Suddenly Elf Dandy said, "Here, help me."

He grabbed Grandy, and with the aid of Mandy and Tandy, gave a big heave-ho and threw him skyward. Grandy bounced on the side of the balloon, slid down and stuck in the hole, filling the space perfectly. Their descent decreased, and they were able to cripple back to the North Pole.

A very disgusted, frigid and agitated Grandy was helped out of the hole. "Why did you throw me in there?" he demanded, brushing the icicles off his backside.

Elf Dandy piped up. "I thought all your grumping and complaining would keep you busy and take your mind off of the cold."

Grandy frowned and then nodded his head. "I see your point. Good thinking."

It was decided never to use the balloon for the investigative trips again.

A private agency was hired to handle the inquiry; one accustomed to snooping, scrounging, and analyzing behavior:

The IRS.

✠ DECEMBER 20 ✳

Mr. Kringle visits the President

On December 20, 1862, Abraham Lincoln was sitting in his office alone, deliberating the fate of young men he had sent to a war not of his making. He was interrupted by a knock on the door.

"Is that you, Mr. Hay?" he asked without budging from his chair.

"It is not Mr. Hay." The voice said no more.

Abraham stood to his feet and creaked toward the door. Opening it, he gazed at a man with a smoky-white beard, stovepipe hat, dressed in the uniform of a colonel in the Union army. "I have two questions for you, Colonel," said Abe. "Who are you and how did you get past my aide?"

"He became distracted by an urgent personal need which called him to the water closet," responded the courtly colonel.

"Well, that answers one."

"For the other answer, I think we should both sit down, sir."

"I am always of a mind to put more pressure on my backside than my feet," Mr. Lincoln smiled, motioning to a chair for his guest and heading for one himself.

The distinguished colonel sat, drew a breath, and began. "Mr. President, I am Kris Kringle."

"Dutch or German?"

"Very."

"Well, Colonel Kringle, you are honored with a fine name."

"I am not a colonel."

"Then you are in danger of being shot for impersonating one. Have you come to assassinate me?"

"Heavens, no. I have come to see you on behalf of the children."

"Children? Are you a father?"

"I hope--many children. Some are black."

"A plantation owner?"

"No, a toyshop."

"Mr. Kringle, I am not partial to riddles, unless they are of my own making."

"Let me speak plainly. I am Santa Claus."

"A little too plainly, dear sir. I must ask you to leave."

"I know it is hard to believe but you are a man of great hope and faith. Stretch that belief for a few moments."

"Speak on. You have until my aide returns to throw you out."

Kris fidgeted in his chair, not sure what he had expected, but definitely discouraged by this beginning. "I have received word, letters, and heard the prayers of black children across the South. They asked me for a Christmas gift-- liberty."

"That is why we are fighting this horrible war. Are you some sort of abolitionist-soothsayer?" Lincoln was perturbed.

"I am what I am, which I declared myself to be. I know you have a proclamation you are about to make law."

"This is common knowledge."

"I also know you are re-considering your decision because people are putting pressure on you to keep slavery out of the issue."

Abraham sat straighter, cleared his throat and said, "Go on."

"Freed children make productive men and women; the kind that build nations."

"Maybe they would be happier back in Africa."

"These children are home. This is their land. They were born here. It is their dream. It is their hope. It is the land where they ask me to come and bring them presents. They are you and you are them."

Lincoln probed the rotund stranger for a glimmer of sanity. Satisfied, he asked, "Well, Santa Claus, if you be, what should this old president do?"

"Be Santa Claus to a whole race of children. Give them what they deserve this Christmas--freedom. They've been good. They have suffered quietly. It is time to let them run and play."

Mr. Lincoln's eyes welled with tears as he nodded his head. Kris Kringle stood to leave. Empty of words, he headed for the door.

"Mr. Claus," Lincoln called, "what do I get for Christmas?" Abe's eyes twinkled in the fading light.

"What do you want?'

"I fancy that stove-pipe hat on your head, dear sir."

"It is yours." Kris handed it to the president.

"Is it magic?" Lincoln probed.

"Everything has its moment of magic," Kris chuckled.

Lincoln smiled. "The children will have their Christmas, Mr. Kringle." Lincoln turned away and stared out the window as Mr. Kringle vanished.

* * * * * * * * * * * * * *

On January 1, 1863, Abraham Lincoln declared the Emancipation Proclamation, freeing the slaves, the law of the land.

****

In the spring of 1865, while riding a horse near enemy lines, President Lincoln was shot at by a sniper, the bullet passing cleanly through his stovepipe hat, leaving him unharmed.

Gunfight at the OhKaye Chorale

OhKaye, Kansas, was named by a man who was in love with a sweet, young lass named Kaye, and wanted to impress her of his noble intentions by buying a town and naming it after her. Shortly after the town was founded and the city hall constructed, the young lady departed, returning to Vassar, and the lovelorn founder moved to Oregon, raising ducks for profit and pleasure, leaving the 924 residents with a hometown, name impaired.

There were motions brought at community meetings to change the name, but some silly excuse, like the terrible cost of printing new stationary, would squelch the effort.

There was one church in town--The OhKaye Community Chapel--922 members. (There was an agnostic couple in town who felt no need for joining.) Although there were 922 members, only 92 souls ever made it to worship services.

This troubled the new, young pastor, this his first post, having just graduated from seminary in Iowa City (that being the one in Iowa.) He believed the church needed to update its approach in order to lure younger people and upscale families. There were 105 younger people in town and approximately 15 upscale families (criteria, more than 3 television sets.)

The young pastor's name was Jon Lennon--no relation to either the Beatle or the Marxist. Pastor Lennon decided to inaugurate his "Hip-Hope" campaign during the Christmas pageant. The young people of the church, all 7 of them, joined with the choir, surnamed the OhKaye Chorale, 19 strong, to comprise a "Rappin', Slappin', Happenin' Christmas Can-Can-Ta-Too". *Silent Night* was replaced with "Born to be Mild" and *Angels We Have Heard on High* became "Whoops, There HE Is".

Rehearsals had been difficult. The bass section, inept at rap, muddled into a dull hum. The sopranos were stiff and nasal toned--Kate Smith meets Aretha Franklin. The tenors screeched out a frightening version of *Joy to the World* by Three Dog Night; then the altos bellowed an off-key version of "I am Woman, Watch Me Grow" as Gabriel talked to Mary, who was wearing bell-bottom jeans and a paisley hemp blouse. Joseph was in leather pants, and instead of a donkey--you guessed it-- a Harley took them to Bethlehem.

Not all of the fine citizens of OhKaye were thrilled with the Reverend's innovative concepts. Boycotts were threatened, but this only caused a greater buzz amongst the 800 souls who never went to the church. There was even rumor that Mr. and Ms. Agnostic might show up for the performance.

Pastor Lennon beamed.

Meanwhile there was a meeting of three deacons--privately. Bill, Ben, and Buck were disturbed. They were brothers and good givers in the tin plate coffers of the Chapel. They decided the whole Christmas presentation was sacrilege and something would have to be done. Well, actually, that's all the further Bill and Ben got. Bill stomped and screamed, Ben talked to Pastor Lennon--no avail-- but Buck . . . well . . . Buck got his shotgun. Now, "he didn't mean no harm", just wanted to get everybody to shut up long enough so he could "convince them of the error of their ways." He decided to make his stand during dress rehearsal.

The OhKaye Chapel was rockin' when Buck drove up, got out of his car, grabbed his double barrel, and headed for the door. Strains of "Oh, Come All You Faithful Dudes" floated outside.

"That's it! I've had it!" Buck flung the door open and charged inside, gun pointed skyward. To his surprise, there were Deacons Jack, Carl, and Baker, standing, six-guns drawn, wearing fake handlebar mustaches and long black coats.

"Baker??" It was all Buck could say.

The three deacons burst into song:

♫ *"We three Earps of Tombstone we be*
  Come to town the baby to see
  For we will guard him
  So Herod cain't harm him
  Let's hear the OhKaye Chorale." ♫

Suddenly there were drums and guitars and the choir singing,

♫ *"OHHH—OHHH--*
  Watch out Jesus, 'ya better run
  Herod's come, he's got a gun.
  Three Earps chase him
  They'll erase him
In Egypt
  You're having fun." ♫

Buck was frozen.

One of the Wise Earps piped up. "Herod, you ain't king no more. There's a new kid in town."

Buck dropped his shotgun. "I give up. You win. I never loaded it anyways. Do your show. I won't be stoppin' 'ya."

Everyone burst into applause.

It was decided to keep Buck's little improvisation in the show.

Opening night was packed. The audience hooted and hollered especially during the "Gunfight at the OhKaye Chorale" section. Buck took big bows. Two Earp mustaches came unglued, but no one really cared.

It was a smash hit. Even the agnostics gave in the offering. Jon Lennon was redeemed from his critics.

Buck reassured everyone, "The gun 'tweren't loaded."

Pastor Lennon closed the show playing his electric guitar, squealing out, "He loves you Yeah! Yeah! Yeah!"

It was silly, but a suitable finale.

Santere and Chenaul

There is nothing warmer than a campfire nor anything more likely to chill the soul with contemplations of inadequacy.

The journey was over, a strange mingling of fulfillment and dread. Santere sat staring into the fire, wondering if any quest would ever come along as delicious and carefree as the one he had just completed. He chuckled, thinking of it. Here he was, a mature man, a ruler of several monastic communities and spiritual orders, chasing a star. To the finite mind it seemed ridiculous. But he had learned several transformations ago--traditional responses garner no newness of life. There must be risk--a chance taken on the potential of greatness, motivated by a stirring in the heart.

What else could he do? There was a star.

No, more an illuminated presence summoning the seeker. He was a seeker. He had led missions to the Great Mountains to commune with the spirits of the wind and trees. Many went cynical, and returned believing. Nature was speaking, compelling us to discover our place in this world.

He had followed the star with five companions: Beloit, a dwarf and student of land mass and rock formations; Pendrick, a warrior philosopher; Sarsan, the great mystique of Kerlon. Then there was Pharlan, his close friend and body servant. And last, the beautiful Chenaul, Quazon to the Teleone people.

As Santere sat in deep thought, he felt a touch on his arm.

"Does the fire speak, my lord?" It was Chenaul.

Santere smiled. "Well it crackles, sizzles, and blows smoke--not that different from some of my council members."

They shared a laugh.

"I couldn't sleep either," she said, finding a place near the fire.

"He was just so beautiful." Santere shivered.

"Santere, he was just a little boy with a face smeared with dates."

"Yes, but what a face."

She nodded. "Will he be protected?"

Santere groaned. "Herod is such a beast and the lad's parents, well, please forgive me, they are peasants."

"Peasants who have come a long way from a carpenter shop."

It was Santere's turn to nod.

"Were we crazy to travel this far?" Chenaul hung her head and snickered.

"I was sitting here wondering the same thing. Chasing a star?"

"A star? How many times did we actually see the star? It was so large and beautiful in the sky back in our homes. Then we set out to follow it and the first thing it did was disappear."

"Behind clouds and mountains. I didn't know what to do."

"Just keep heading west, faithfully."

"And then it would appear again, luring, taunting us on."

Chenaul sat to her knees, turning towards Santere. "No, it wasn't a taunt--more a wink. I could almost hear its musical voice drawing us on 'Are you still with me, pilgrims?'"

"It was such a long journey."

"Twenty-three cycles of the moon."

"It would have been quicker if I hadn't stopped off in Cardis to help negotiate that treaty between the Morias and the Nadors."

"You were brilliant. They thought you were a god."

Santere looked at her. They gazed deeply, the way lovers remember the exact moment they fell in love.

"I am no god." Santere broke the tension.

"Jesus."

"A boy, a very natural little boy."

"It was worth the journey." Chenaul scooted forward but also closer. "What will come of him?"

"We are an adoring, needy, and ignorant race. He will be adored, meet the needs of thousands, and ultimately be judged by the ignorant."

"I fear for him."

"Today he plays with those toys you brought."

"He certainly was more interested in them than the gold, frankincense and myrrh," Chenaul giggled. Her laugh--so sweet and infectious.

Santere laughed. "I thought I would die when he asked if he could eat the frankincense."

"A practical lad. You wouldn't want a king to be scattered and foolish."

"A king? Is that little Bedouin boy a king? Are we the foolish ones, Chenaul?"

"You called me by name. You rarely do."

"I think not. . ."

"No, it's usually 'milady' or 'Your Highness'."

"Oh, I didn't know."

"And I don't know if we saw a king or a little boy. The star says he has an arc to greatness."

They sat quietly until sleep overcame them, and then drifted away, closer than ever.

They returned to the Great Mountains, in love--with life, stars, travels, Jesus, and. . . . each other.

They married, bore a son and named him Apollos.

When Apollos was grown he journeyed to Greece, where he met Saul of Tarsus, a follower of the Prophet of the Star.

Santere and Chenaul's son spent the rest of his life honoring and witnessing about his mother and father's dream and the message of THE STAR CHILD.

🎁 DECEMBER 23 🎁

'Twas the Night Before the Night

'Twas the night before the night

And all through the shop

Nothing dare move

From bottom to top.

The toys are all stacked

So neatly in bags

Labeled and ready

With holiday tags.

The reindeer are fed

And safe in their bed

With visions of flying
And the journey ahead.

Each elf found his space

His own special place

To sleep the night away

Preparing for the day

When they polish and shine

Till all is sparkling and fine

Then Santa will say

"Elves, load up my sleigh!"

So ascending into the sky

With reindeer yearning to fly

And deliver a special toy

For a precious girl or boy.

To return within the night
Just like a burst of light

And start it all anew

More gifts for me and you.

'Twas the night before the night

And all through our mind

Are visions of tomorrow

And what we will find.

We thank you Santa

As we gladly receive

The blessing of giving

On this Christmas Eve.

▣ DECEMBER 24 ▣

Mrs. Kringle's Little Secret

Mr. Kringle was worried. (As much as a Santa Claus can be worried and maintain his jolly persona.) It was his wife, Katerina. She was different. Well, she was always a little different, which is why he loved her. Yet this difference was different in such a different way. He couldn't quite put his finger on it. Once when he walked in the room, he found her talking with one of the elves. She stopped, looked up, smiled, and said, "Well, hell-o, Santa Claus." She never called him Santa Claus, except in formal occasions, and how many of those do you have at the North Pole toyshop?

There was more evidence.

She was nervous, in a busy twitty way-- fidgety, that's it; sorta flitting about like a bumblebee at a florist convention.

And she was too nice.

She was always nice, but this was like "nice in a can" that someone sprays in a room so you will notice the "nice" spray.

Mr. Kringle was perplexed and annoyed.

He asked her what was wrong but she just smirked and said, "Well, what would you mean, Claus man? I am fine."

And of course, she said it NICELY.

Santa tried to interrogate some of the elves, but they played stupid. (Very well, may I add . . .)

She had a secret. He *hated* it when she had a secret. He shuddered as he recalled past secrets. There was the time she purchased a treadmill, trying to get in better shape. She slipped, fell on her face and broke her nose. Then she became convinced that he, the Claus, needed to lose weight, so she baked sugar-free cookies laced with diet pills. Before he could taste them, Elf Wandi ate a half-dozen and nearly disappeared. (Elves don't have much body fat!) Then there was the time she thought the reindeer needed costumes, so she knitted and crocheted for three months making each one a special outfit, only to find on Christmas Eve, she had forgotten to put holes for the legs and hooves.

They wore them as antler hats.

Mr. Kringle remembered well. Thus, worried.

He fussed and searched for hidden surprises, trying to discover Mrs. Kringle's secret. It was to no avail.

Finally he decided to ask. "Katerina, really, what is going on?"

"Santa, what could you mean?"

"Don't call me Santa. You never call me Santa."

"Surely I do. That's your name--Santa Claus."

"I know my name. But you always call me Kris, or Mr. Kringle..."

"Or schnucky-cuddly--wumkins." She tickled his chin.

He laughed, and then cleared his throat, "Don't change the subject."

"I didn't. We were talking about names."

"Why are you being so weird?"

"Weird?"

She was not going to make it easy.

Mr. Kringle pursued. "You're polite, nice, and kind. What's wrong with you?"

"These are bad things?"

"You know what I mean. A little nice is nice but a lot of nice is . . .well . . .not so nice."

"Are you feeling all right, Santa?" She reached for his forehead.

"Don't Santa, me. I know what I know, so don't tell me I don't know, if you know what I mean?"

"No."

"What are you hiding? What's the secret?"

"I love you, but that's no secret," she winked.

"Stop trying to be nice."

"If you wish. I will attempt to be meaner."

"Katerina, stop toying with me."

"That's funny--toying with Santa Claus--what else would I do?"

Even a grumpy Claus had to laugh at that. A moment passed and he spoke again. "Really, what is going on?"

She knew he was serious. It was no time to play or be evasive. "I wanted to keep it a secret."

"A-ha! I knew it."

"Would you stop gloating and listen? You know how sometimes I have fears . . ."

"Which one? Would it be talking dolls that say 'Mommy' . . ."

"They give me the willies."

"Or carrots?'

"They are orange and pointy."

"Or maybe green striped candy canes?"

"You got to admit, that's creepy."

He chuckled. "Did I miss any?"

"Yeah, the big one."

Santa frowned. "Katerina, we agreed not to discuss that one."

"I'm not discussing. You asked."

"We worked that out long ago. I understand."

"But I don't."

They both sat for a long breath, looking at the ground. Man and wife realized the problem.

Katerina Kringle was afraid of heights.

Kris had wished for her to accompany him on the Christmas Eve journey, but she was too afraid of flying with the sleigh and the reindeer. It had been discussed and decided. She would never go. Though lonely for her presence, he pressed on.

She broke the silence. "I knew how much it meant to you, so I asked the elves to help me."

"The elves? What would an elf know about height?"

She continued. "First I climbed up on a box, then the stairs, and finally they took me up in our hot-air-balloon."

"You mean "Kris' Tires" Balloon? That thing is not safe!"

"But I did it. I made it, Kris. I didn't scream or holler or beg to be taken down or even throw up."

"Well, that's good," Kris inserted uncomfortably.

"I want to go with you."

"Are you sure?"

"Yes, I'm sure."

He kissed her the way a brave woman should be kissed.

That Christmas Katerina Kringle flew in the stars--a little headachy, dizzy, giddy, worried, nervous, and faint--but she flew.

It was a better Christmas than Mr. Kringle could ever remember.

And best of all . . . she didn't throw up!

DECEMBER 25

Morning Has Woken

Morning has woken! The silence finally broken!

Twisted shafts of heavy-laden gray-borne light permeating the room with shadowy visitors: once a chair, a shirt, and a dresser, now ominous and foreboding--unknown. An evening's impasse of tossing and turning, wanting to sleep, needing the rest, but images and dreams and chunks of childhood giddy hopes invade the mind, dispelling all efforts to slumber.

The thoughts chink and clank like boxcars, vying for space. What will she think? Does he know what I got him? What's in the big red, glittery box with the calico bow; the one for me that I don't know? Is it what I asked for, or a surprise from an ingenious friend who noticed me staring longingly at that 'something' which I relinquished—never mind.

Sleep is fruitless-- such a fragile state, disturbed by the slightest notion, or the least important thought-intrusion.

There--more light. Look! It is a chair, not a hulking wolf; a dresser, not a Sherman tank. Meanwhile, the sun plays games of tic-tac-toe on the frosty windowpane as a slight chill shivers the room.

Pull up the covers--shudder--BRRR-- such raging fun.

Morning has woken! The silence finally broken!

The children stir and wiggle, emitting a glorious giggle.

They are like foam in a soda can on a hot summer's day--ready to fizz and explode--just touch it, snap its top--watch it erupt; gurgling and gushing, spraying energy in all directions.

What to wear, I don't care. Slipping on the loosest garment, brushing the hair, rubbing a tooth or two with some fragrant paste.

The children are whispering. They know I'm awake. The wait will soon be over--the taste of dreams fills the soul with an explosion of anticipation.

Soon--a word filled with two nothings, indefinable.

I come to their door, more giggling.

"Let me go see if Santa has come," I speak through the door with morning's crackle in my voice.

They say nothing, but I feel their yearning pound through the door--HURRY! HURRY!

Coming down the stairs, feeling the soft carpet caress my toes, everything is energized by the moment's exaggeration. Then--there it is. A hazy glimmering glow of festive lights barely illuminating a stockpile of gleaming and glistening presents, as the bicycle for Bryan radiates its own light-force from a position near the tree, and a plate of crumbled cookies lay next to a nearly empty glass of milk, with chocolate lip marks pressed on the rim.

There is the smell of candy mingled with the warmth and heat of furnaced-air meshing with a vision of color and texture of rainbow sherbet dancing before the eyes--so satisfying.

Morning has woken! The silence is broken!

It's time to call the family to celebrate our love beneath the tree!

MERRY CHRISTMAS TO US ALL!

Acknowledgements

Editor: Janet Scott
Art direction: Angela Cring
Art Design: Tracy Eustice, Priceless Productions
Research: Dollie Cring
Layout: Word Mill, Nashville, Tenn.
Son of Santa: Russ Cring

Special Thanks to:
Printing Etc. and Justin Michael Scott for his story
"Bagley"

LWS Publishers
227 Bayshore Drive
Hendersonville, Tennessee 37075
(800) 643-4718 ext. 74
Fax: (615) 826-3883
i n f o @ c l a z z y . c o m